GAIL GIBBONS

MY BASEBALL BOOK

HarperCollins**Publishers**

Special thanks to Fawn Carter, physical
education instructor, Waits River Valley
School, Corinth, Vermont

My Baseball Book
Copyright © 2000 by Gail Gibbons

Manufactured in China.
All rights reserved.
For information address HarperCollins Children's Books,
a division of HarperCollins Publishers,
10 East 53rd Street, New York, NY 10022.
http://www.harperchildrens.com

Library of Congress Cataloging-in-Publication Data
Gibbons, Gail.
My baseball book / by Gail Gibbons.
p. cm.
Summary: An introduction to baseball,
describing the equipment, playing field,
rules, players, and process of the game.
ISBN 0-688-17137-0
1. Baseball Juvenile literature.   [1. Baseball.]
I. Title.   GV867.5.G53 2000   796.357—dc21   99-32945   CIP

10 11 12 13 SCP 20 19 18 17 16 15 14
❖

Baseball is fun, whether you are playing yourself or rooting for your favorite team.

BASEBALL CAP

BASEBALL

BASEBALL GLOVE,
also called a MITT

To play, you need a ball, a bat, and gloves . . .

BAT

BATTING HELMET

PROTECTIVE GEAR
for the CATCHER
and UMPIRE

BASEBALL SHOES with
spikes called CLEATS

and sometimes a uniform.

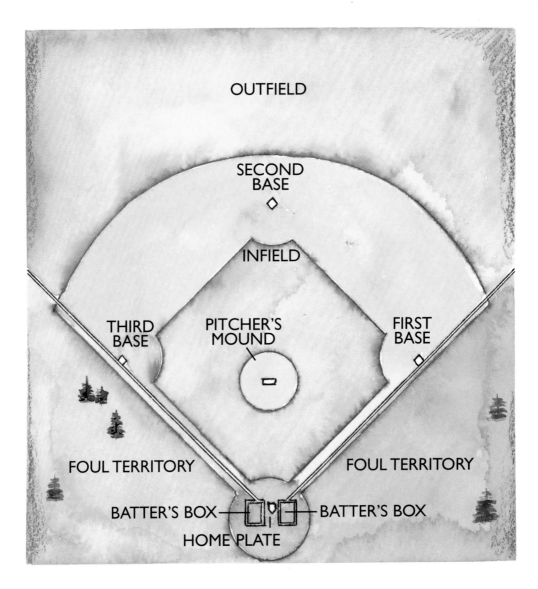

A baseball field is sometimes called a diamond.

THE ROBINS

THE OWLS

There are usually nine players on a team. These players try to score the most runs for their team. To score, a player must advance to first base, second base, and third base, then back to home plate. That's a run!

Each team gets three outs in its half of an inning.

| | 1 | 2 | 3 | 4 | 5 | 6 | 7 | 8 | 9 | 10 | TOTAL |

VISITORS

HOME

HOME TEAM

VISITING TEAM

A baseball game usually lasts for nine innings. Games for younger players are often shorter. Each inning has a top half and a bottom half. The visiting team bats first, at the top of the inning.

Coaches teach the players. They also choose the batting order and decide which player will play which position.

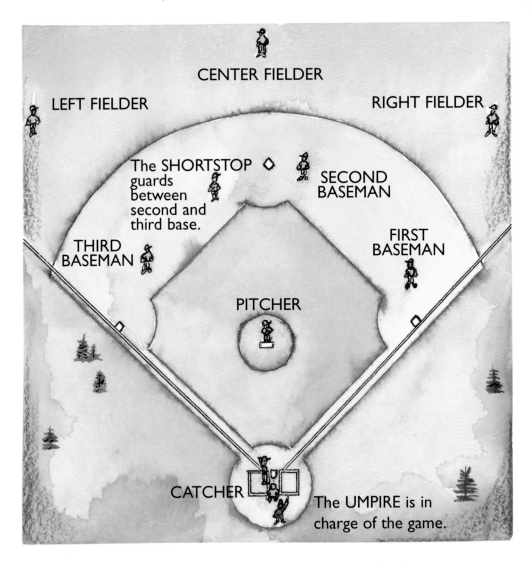

CENTER FIELDER

LEFT FIELDER

RIGHT FIELDER

The SHORTSTOP guards between second and third base.

SECOND BASEMAN

THIRD BASEMAN

FIRST BASEMAN

PITCHER

CATCHER

The UMPIRE is in charge of the game.

The home team takes the field, and the umpire yells, "Play ball!"

It is also a strike if the batter doesn't swing but the ball passes through the STRIKE ZONE.

The first batter steps to the plate. The pitcher winds up and throws the ball toward the catcher. She wants to get that batter out! One way is to strike him out. It's a strike if the batter swings and misses.

On the first pitch, the batter swings and misses. On the second pitch, the batter hits the ball into foul territory.

Three strikes and the batter will be out! But he hits the third pitch toward the shortstop and runs for first base.

The shortstop catches the ball and throws it to first. If the first baseman has her foot on the bag and catches the ball before the runner gets there, the runner is out.

It's a close play, but the runner makes it to first base before the ball gets there. He's safe.

If the pitcher throws four balls out of the strike zone, that's a WALK.

The pitcher throws four balls out of the strike zone to the next batter. The batter goes to first base, and the runner on first advances to second base. Then the third batter gets a hit.

Now there are runners on all three bases—the bases are loaded. The fourth batter swings, and it's another hit! The runner on third races to touch home plate. The visiting team scores a run!

The next batter hits a fly ball that is caught in the outfield. That means the batter is out.

The visiting team leads, 1 to 0.

When three batters are out, it's the other team's turn to hit. The visiting team takes the field, and the home team steps up to bat. It's the bottom of the first inning.

One . . .

two . . .

three . . .

four . . .

five innings are played.

By the sixth inning, the visiting team is ahead by three runs.

It's the bottom of the sixth—the home team's last turn at bat. There are two outs, and the bases are loaded. The fans hold their breath.

The final score is 9 to 8.

The pitcher winds up and throws. The batter swings. And it's a home run! One...two...three...four runners cross home plate. The home team wins. Everyone cheers. It's been such a good game.

MY BASEBALL GLOSSARY

 ball: a pitch outside the strike zone

 defense: working to prevent runs, by throwing good pitches, catching batted balls, and other means

 fly ball: a batted ball that is hit in the air; if it's caught before it hits the ground, it's an out

 foul ball: a batted ball that goes outside the foul lines

 hit: a batted ball that is hit into fair territory and allows the batter to make it to base

 offense: working to score runs, by getting hits, running the bases, and other means

 run: one point, earned each time a player touches all three bases and crosses home plate without being called out

 sportsmanship: playing fairly and enjoying a game, no matter who wins or loses

 strike: a pitch that the batter swings at and misses or hits foul, or that crosses home plate within the strike zone

 teamwork: playing together as a team, encouraging and supporting all of your teammates

 walk: a base on balls, in which the batter goes to first base after the pitcher throws four balls out of the strike zone

 Kinds of Baseball Teams
Tee Ball: a version of baseball, especially for children under eight, in which batters swing at a ball placed on a tee, rather than thrown from a pitcher

 Little League: a baseball league for children between the ages of eight and twelve

 Major Leagues: the highest-level league for professional baseball players